# Rosie Runs Away

*by Maryann Macdonald*
*Illustrated by Melissa Sweet*

ATHENEUM     1990     NEW YORK

For Joan, who ran away
—M.M.

To my folks, with love
—M.S.

Text copyright © 1990 by Maryann Macdonald
Illustrations copyright © 1990 by Melissa Sweet

Atheneum
Macmillan Publishing Company
866 Third Avenue, New York, NY 10022
Collier Macmillan Canada, Inc.
First Edition
Printed in Hong Kong by South China Printing Co.

A LUCAS-EVANS BOOK

10  9  8  7  6  5  4  3  2  1

Library of Congress Cataloging-in-Publication Data
Macdonald, Maryann.
    Rosie runs away/by Maryann Macdonald; illustrated by Melissa Sweet.—1st ed.   p.   cm.
    "A Lucas-Evans book"
    Summary: When her mother chastises her for taking her little brother out on a blueberry-picking adventure, Rosie decides to run away.
    ISBN 0-689-31625-9
    [1. Runaways—Fiction.  2. Brothers and sisters—Fiction.  3. Family life—Fiction.]  I. Sweet, Melissa, ill.  II. Title.
PZ7.M1486Ro  1990  [E]—dc20  89-27575  CIP  AC

Rosie wanted to bake with Mama.
But Mama was busy.
Busy with Mat.

That Fat Mat.
She fed him.
She washed him.
She dressed him.
And she put him to bed.

"Let's bake now, Mama,"
said Rosie.

"Rosie," said Mama,
"I'm tired.
I need to rest.
Maybe we'll bake later."

But Fat Mat would not fall asleep.
He jumped up and down
on his bed.
"Mom, Mom, Ma!" he yelled.

Rosie went to his door.
"Shhh!" she said.
"Mama's tired."
"Wosie!" yelled Fat Mat.
He held out his arms to her.

So Rosie lifted Fat Mat out of bed.
She took him out of the room,
down the hall, and out the back door.
She took him outside to play,
so that Mama could rest.

She showed him how to make mud pies.
"Mmmmmm," said Fat Mat.
"No, no," said Rosie.
"You can't eat mud pies."
Fat Mat started to cry.

So Rosie took Fat Mat
over to a blueberry bush.
She set him down under a big
clump of berries.
"Mmmmmm!" said Fat Mat again.
He liked berries.

Rosie got her bucket
and started to pick blueberries.
She picked the biggest and the best.
Then she put them all into her bucket
for a surprise for Mama.

Fat Mat rubbed his eyes.
He was tired.
So Rosie showed Fat Mat her secret
hiding place under the porch.
It was dark and cool and quiet.

Fat Mat crawled in.
He lay down and fell sound asleep.
So did Rosie.

"Rosie! Mat!"
Rosie heard Mama's voice calling them.
She crawled out from under the porch.
"Here we are, Mama!" she called.

But Mama did not seem happy
to see them.
"Rosie!" said Mama.
"Where have you been?"
"I took Fat Mat outside,"
said Rosie, "so that you could rest."
"You should never take Mat out
without asking me," said Mama.
"Just look at him!"
Rosie looked at Fat Mat.

His face was blue.
His pajamas were blue.
And he was covered with mud.

"We made mud pies," said Rosie.
But Mama did not answer.
"And we picked blueberries," said Rosie.
"See? I picked all these for you!"
But Mama still did not answer.
She carried Fat Mat back inside.

Mama washed him again.
She dressed him again.
And she put him back to bed.
"Now, Rosie," said Mama,
"go to your room and play quietly."

So Rosie went to her room.
But she did not play quietly.
She got her pajamas
and her doll and her candy.
She put them in a bag.

And she tiptoed quietly
out the door.

Mama did not need her,
so Rosie was running away.
She walked out the garden gate.

She walked over the bridge.
And she sat down
under a weeping willow tree.

From under the willow tree
Rosie could see her house,
but she was sure
Mama could not see her.

No one would find her there.
She could live there alone forever.
Mama would not miss her.
Mama was too busy with Fat Mat.

But what about Daddy?
Who would tell Daddy jokes?
When Daddy came home tired,
Rosie told him jokes.
"That's my Rosie-Posie,"
Daddy always said.
He would miss Rosie.

And what about Fat Mat?
Who would play with him?
When he was bored and fussy,
who would play peek-a-boo?
Who would tickle his tummy?
Fat Mat would miss Rosie.

Maybe Mama did not need Rosie.
But Daddy did.
And Fat Mat did.

Rosie stood up.
She packed her things.
And she walked back home.

Fat Mat was still asleep.
But Mama was in the kitchen.
She smiled at Rosie.
"I've washed all the blueberries
you picked," she said.
"Will you help me bake some pies?"

Rosie smiled back.
"Yes," she said.
"I'll help you bake some pies."

So they made one big pie
for Mama and Daddy.
They made one small pie
for Rosie.
And they made one tiny little pie
for Fat Mat.